MEET ALL THESE FRIENDS IN BUZZ BOOKS:

Thomas the Tank Engine
The Animals of Farthing Wood
Fireman Sam
Joshua Jones
Looney Tunes
Babar
Rupert
Flintstones
Bugs Bunny
James Bond Junior

This presentation first published in 1993 by Buzz Books,
an imprint of Reed Children's Books
Michelin House, 81 Fulham Road, London SW3 6RB
and Auckland, Melbourne, Singapore and Toronto

First published in France under the title *Babar et ce Coquin d'Arthur*
First published in Great Britain in 1948 by
Methuen & Co Ltd
Copyright © Librairie Hachette 1946
This presentation copyright © 1993 Reed International Books Limited

ISBN 1 85591 316X

Printed in Italy by LEGO

BABAR

and that Rascal Arthur

LAURENT DE BRUNHOFF

Babar the King and Queen Celeste were
tired after a year of hard work and they set
out with their children for a holiday by the
sea. Here they are at Celesteville Station.

Pom, Flora, Alexander and Zephir the
monkey climbed up to the overhead car.
Babar's cousin, Arthur, wanted to go with
them, but Babar said he was too big now.

During the journey, the three little
elephants looked out of their windows
and Arthur made faces at them from
down below. It was great fun.

Babar had taken a house at
Baribarbotton. When they arrived the
children ran on ahead, very excited.

"Isn't the sea lovely!" Celeste cried
contentedly, "and the house looks so nice!"

Arthur had a plan of his own and slipped
away while Zephir and the other children
went shrimping. Flora found some crabs.

"Come and see
my beautiful
earrings!" she
called to her
brothers. But
when Zephir
took hold of
one, it pinched
him and hurt.
His skin was
not as tough
as an elephant's.

But where was Arthur all this time?

He had found what he was after – the
great airfield nearby.

"This is more interesting than fishing!"
he thought.

Arthur had never seen so many
aeroplanes at one time before. The best one
of all was a green one. He longed to climb
up on its tail.

And what happened next? Elephants rushed onto the field to see the big green aeroplane take off . . . with Arthur on its tail.

He had just clambered up there when the plane began to move. He was terrified, but dared not jump. He clung on for dear life. First one, then another, of the elephants caught sight of him.

They all began to shout:
"He's going to fall! He's going to fall!"
Soon all they could see was a tiny spot of
red on the aeroplane. "Come on," said the
elephants. "We'd better go and
inform the King at once.
He'll be on the beach."

17

The pilot of the aeroplane threw out
a parachute, and Arthur managed to put
it on. Then he jumped. At first he fell like
a stone. Then the parachute opened. It
was fun – until a strong wind blew him
far, far from Baribarbotton.

18

The kangaroos took him to the station to catch a train home. They said over and over again, "You will come back, won't you, Mr Elephant?"

"Perhaps," Arthur replied. He was sorry to leave these nice new friends.

22

When the train came, it was not meant
for elephants, so Arthur had to travel in a
truck. Soon he fell fast asleep.

They came to a forest where little
monkeys often used to drop from the trees
to the roof of the trains for a ride. When
they saw Arthur, they cried: "Look what's
here! Let's play a trick on him!" And those
mischievous animals unhitched his truck.

"Oh dear, oh dear!" Arthur wailed when he woke up. "Now what has happened?"

He walked till he came to the bank of a river, where he met two dromedaries.

"Good day," he said. "My name is Arthur. I am the little cousin of Babar, King of the Elephants. Could you take me to Baribarbotton? I'm lost."

The dromedaries replied that they would
be delighted to take Arthur if he could think
of a way to cross the river, which was full of
crocodiles. Luckily a nice fat hippopotamus
and his brother offered to help.

And there, in no time, was a bridge of

hippopotamuses. The crocodiles were furious!

Over the river, the three travellers plunged into the desert and kept going until evening, when they rested.

The next day was very hot. At length they came to an Arab village. Arthur was terribly thirsty. He had to find water.

An old man showed him where he could find a well. Arthur was just finishing his second bucketful when he saw Babar at the end of the street, running towards him!

28

Babar was so pleased to have found
Arthur that he did not scold him much. They
drove back to Baribarbotton. When they
reached the seashore, Babar sounded his
horn and the whole family rushed to meet
them.

"There you are, at last!" cried Zephir.
"Typical Arthur!"